'Tom's Den' and 'The Big Trick'
An original concept by Jenny Jinks
© Jenny Jinks

Illustrated by Jo Byatt

Published by MAVERICK ARTS PUBLISHING LTD
Studio 11, City Business Centre, 6 Brighton Road,
Horsham, West Sussex, RH13 5BB
© Maverick Arts Publishing Limited November 2019
+44 (0)1403 256941

A CIP catalogue record for this book is available at the British Library.

ISBN 978-1-84886-621-8

www.maverickbooks.co.uk

Pink

This book is rated as: Pink Band (Guided Reading)
This story is decodable at Letters and Sounds Phase 2.

Tom's Den

and

The Big Trick

By **Jenny Jinks**   Illustrated by
Jo Byatt

The Letter D

Trace the lower and upper case letter with a finger. Sound out the letter.

*Around,
up,
down*

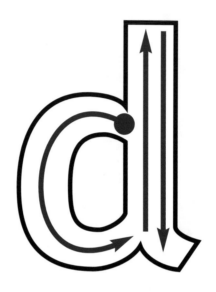

*Down,
up,
around*

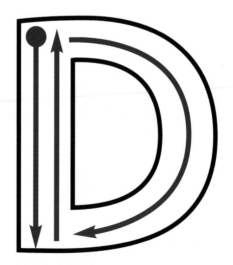

Some words to familiarise:

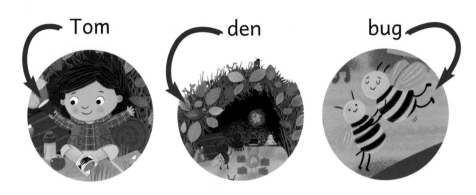

Tom   den   bug

High-frequency words:

a   has   in   his   go   of   no

Tips for Reading 'Tom's Den'

- Practise the words listed above before reading the story.

- If the reader struggles with any of the other words, ask them to look for sounds they know in the word. Encourage them to sound out the words and help them read the words if necessary.

- After reading the story, ask the reader why Tom moved to a different den.

Fun Activity

Build your own den with blankets!

Tom's Den

Tom has a den.

Tom has a bug in his den.

9

Tom has a big bug in his den.

Tom has lots of bugs in his den.

13

Tom has no den.

Tom has a big den.

The Letter T

Trace the lower and upper case letter with a finger. Sound out the letter.

*Down,
lift,
cross*

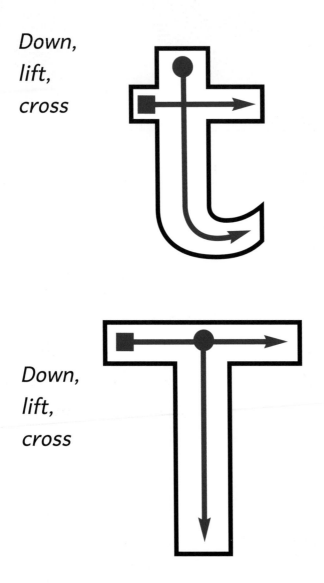

*Down,
lift,
cross*

Some words to familiarise:

carrot   hat   rabbit

High-frequency words:

a put in the no is

Tips for Reading 'The Big Trick'

- Practise the words listed above before reading the story.

- If the reader struggles with any of the other words, ask them to look for sounds they know in the word. Encourage them to sound out the words and help them read the words if necessary.

- After reading the story, ask the reader how the carrot and the rabbit disappeared.

Fun Activity

Discuss other magic tricks that Tom could do.

The Big Trick

Tom puts a carrot in the hat.

Tip, tap.

23

Tom puts a rabbit in the hat.

Tip, tap.

Tom is sad.

Book Bands for Guided Reading

The Institute of Education book banding system is a scale of colours that reflects the various levels of reading difficulty. The bands are assigned by taking into account the content, the language style, the layout and phonics. Word, phrase and sentence level work is also taken into consideration.

Maverick Early Readers are a bright, attractive range of books covering the pink to white bands. All of these books have been book banded for guided reading to the industry standard and edited by a leading educational consultant.

To view the whole Maverick Readers scheme, visit our website at
www.maverickearlyreaders.com

Or scan the QR code above to view our scheme instantly!